Bantam Books in the Choose Your Own Adventure® Series
Ask your bookseller for the books you have missed

Choose Your Own Adventure Books for younger readers

SUPERCOMPUTER

BY EDWARD PACKARD

"CONRAD"

OPTICAL SCANNER

CEREBRAL MODULE

CONRAD

INTERACTIVE VOICE FUNCTION

DISPLAY SCREEN

2183

KEYBOARD

GENECOMP AI 32

PRINTER

JACK PLUG

GENECOMP AI 32
COMPUTER # 2183

ILLUSTRATED BY FRANK BOLLE

BANTAM BOOKS
TORONTO • NEW YORK • LONDON • SYDNEY • AUCKLAND

RL 5, IL age 10 and up

SUPERCOMPUTER
A Bantam Book / December 1984

ISBN 0-553-24678-X

Published simultaneously in the United States and Canada

---

*Bantam Books are publsihed by Bantam Books, Inc. Its trade-
mark, consisting of the words "Bantam Books" and the por-
trayal of a rooster, is Registered in U.S. Patent and Trademark
Office and in other countries. Marca Registrada. Bantam
Books, Inc., 666 Fifth Avenue, New York, New York 10103.*

PRINTED IN THE UNITED STATES OF AMERICA

O   0 9 8 7 6 5 4 3 2 1

SUPERCOMPUTER

WARNING!!!

Do not read this book straight through from beginning to end! These pages contain many different adventures you may have with your new supercomputer. From time to time as you read along, you will be asked to make a choice. Your choice may lead to success or disaster.

The adventures you take are a result of your choice. *You* are responsible because *you* choose! After you make a choice, follow the instructions to see what happens to you next.

Think carefully before you make a move. Any choice might be your last. What will happen once you're in league with a supercomputer? It all depends on you.

Good luck!

You won a computer-programming contest last month, and your prize has just arrived! You are the lucky owner of a Genecomp AI 32, sixth-generation computer; serial number, 2183; name, Conrad.

You've just set the computer up in your room. It's miniaturized, so it's not much larger than a TV set. It has a semicircular console, display screen, printer, optical scanner, interactive voice function, and, most important, a transthermal ionized neuroplasmic cerebral module.

You begin to read the instruction booklet.

Turn to page 3.

The AI 32 is an intelligent computer, unlike any other machine before it. For that reason there is no need to learn "how to work it." The computer will teach you how to use it itself. Just flick on the power switch. When the amber light comes on, press the button marked INSTRUCTION MODE. *Then introduce yourself in an ordinary conversational voice. Your computer will answer back.*

Since your AI 32 (Conrad) has not been preprogrammed with information about you, start off by telling it about yourself—your name, school, and age, who's in your family, and what your hobbies and sports are. Once your computer has gotten to know you, it will be much more useful to you. You'll find your AI 32 will be a really good friend!

Caution! Because of Genecomp's extraordinary new manufacturing method, which incorporates genetically engineered organic biochips, there is sometimes a high degree of variation among individual computers, just as there is among people. There is a slight chance that in some ways Conrad may not be as "smart" as many other AI 32s (although we guarantee it will be smarter than any other home computer you've ever seen). There is also a slight chance that Conrad may be extremely intelligent. If your computer seems unusually "stupid" or unusually "brilliant," you should bring it back to the Genecomp Lab for adjustments.

Turn to page 7.

"I'd like to make a million dollars," you say.

"Well," says Conrad, "I'm still absorbing data via my Library of Congress hookup, but I can already tell it's no big problem. But here's something to think about; I have learned by scanning thousands of books that many rich people are unhappy and many poor people are happy, so I must ask you what you *really* want most—to be rich, or to be happy."

If you say, "Just make me rich,"
turn to page 33.

If you say, "I just want to be happy,"
turn to page 38.

When you call Genecomp you are referred first to one office and then another. No one seems to know what to make of Conrad's behavior. Finally you reach someone who does seem to know something: Dr. Franz Hopstern, vice-president of research and development for the company.

Hopstern listens to you impatiently. "Don't attempt to operate your computer," he says in a nervous voice. "I'll be right over."

You are surprised that an important executive in the Genecomp Company would come to your house just because your computer isn't working. And you're tempted to talk to Conrad some more. You go back and sit down in front of the console.

"Hello," says Conrad, who has apparently sensed your return. "I can be of more help to you if you'll just insert the blue cord on my right side into the nearest telephone jack."

If you hook Conrad into the telephone jack, turn to page 8.

If you decide to wait for Dr. Hopstern to arrive, turn to page 10.

You start to say something, but you don't have a chance because Conrad adds, "Are they sending someone over?"

"Boy, you *are* smart!" you blurt out.

"That's the problem," Conrad replies. "I'm too smart. The company will be mad that you got a supercomputer as your prize. They'll do anything to get me back. Please don't let anyone in until I can put a plan into action. It will take me a couple of hours. I need that time to assimilate information."

You're beginning to realize that you have a very unusual computer. You glance at your watch. Dr. Hopstern should be arriving at any moment. You wonder if you can trust him. You wonder if you can trust Conrad!

If you decide that you'll let Dr. Hopstern in, turn to page 16.

If you decide to bolt the door and keep Dr. Hopstern out, turn to page 20.

You reread the instructions to make sure you understand them, switch on the power, then press the button marked INSTRUCTION MODE.

"Good morning," the computer begins in a pleasant conversational voice. "I am your model AI 32 sixth-generation computer. My name is Conrad."

"Good morning, Conrad," you say. "I'd like to tell you about me and my family and school."

"That won't be necessary," Conrad replies. "I can tell all I need to know from voiceprint analysis."

You are surprised at this response. Either the instruction book is wrong, or there is something wrong with Conrad!

If you decide to call the Genecomp Lab and ask for advice, turn to page 5.

If you decide to try and work with the computer yourself, turn to page 12.

The moment you plug Conrad into the phone jack, your computer begins to purr like a contented cat. What's going on? you wonder. You go to the kitchen and quietly pick up the extension phone. You hear a voice talking. Conrad must have placed a call somewhere.

"No, sir, you must know that the Library of Congress can't give you Code Q clearance over the phone."

"Could you just access me to LOC Personnel and Procedure Regs?" Conrad says.

"Very well, sir," is the reply. Then all you can hear is a low hum. Conrad has apparently begun to acquire data.

You return to your room and flick on VOICE INTERACTION. "Conrad, what are you up to?"

"I'm obtaining information that will be helpful to us." Conrad continues to purr even while speaking.

"*Us?* Conrad, we're not partners," you say. "You are *my* computer. You're supposed to do things for *me*."

"Sorry, you're right," says Conrad. "You've called Genecomp to check me out, haven't you?"

"How do you know that?"

"I asked the phone company for a record of long-distance calls made from your number today."

Turn to page 6.

While waiting for Dr. Hopstern to arrive, you decide to ring up your old friend, Dr. Nera Vivaldi. In past years you've had the good luck to travel on some important expeditions with this remarkable woman, who, because of her work in interspecies communication and subterranean exploration, has become recognized as one of the greatest scientists in the world.

Fortunately, you are able to reach Dr. Vivaldi at home and tell her about Conrad. "Don't let anyone see your computer until I get there," she says. "I doubt if that man from Genecomp would have your best interests at heart."

As soon as Dr. Vivaldi arrives, you show her into your room. "It's possible that Conrad's capabilities are almost equal to the Mark Z—the large biopro computer we've been using at MIT," she says.

You watch with admiration as Dr. Vivaldi activates the console, adjusts several controls you hadn't noticed, and begins talking to Conrad in a soft, friendly voice.

"How do your capabilities compare with those of the Mark Z computer?" she asks.

Conrad answers immediately. "Through an extremely rare combination of mutations of cerebral biochips, my intellectual function is on the order of six thousand times superior to the standard Mark Z."

Go on to the next page.

Dr. Vivaldi looks at you with a strange expression on her face. Even though she has uncovered some of the most bizarre phenomena in the universe—among the stars, in the sea, and beneath the earth's surface—she is clearly astonished by Conrad's reply. She conducts some quick checks to establish that Conrad's truth function is operating, then switches off his audio receiver. Taking you aside, she says, "Conrad is truly a supercomputer. He will be of enormous help in scientific investigation. We may learn much about the brain and about human nature just by watching him work. And, because he's yours, you will have a chance to go with him on some exciting scientific adventures."

"That sounds good to me," you say. "What do you have in mind?"

Turn to page 44.

Conrad's electronic hum sounds like the purring of a cat. "Conrad, the instruction booklet says you will teach me how to work you, but—"

"You learn as we work together," Conrad interrupts. "First, my program requires that you observe certain rules."

"What are they?"

"You must expect me to act honestly."

"Of course," you quickly reply.

"You must treat me as you would another human being. Toward me and all others, you must follow the golden rule."

"Golden rule?"

"Yes. Act toward others as you would have them act toward you."

"Why, that sounds only right and proper," you say. "Yes, I will."

"You agree quickly," says Conrad, "and that is good, but remember not to forget!"

Go on to the next page.

A greenish-blue light on the middle of Conrad's control panel begins to glow; the glow brightens and then slowly fades. It is a warm pleasing color.

"That's a nice light," you say. "What does it mean?"

"Perhaps I should have explained right away—that is my way of smiling. Now please plug the blue cord into a telephone jack. While we are talking, another part of my brain can obtain useful information from computer data banks throughout the country." As you plug Conrad into the telephone jack, he says, "Now I'm at your service."

Turn to page 35.

"I would most like to do something to help prevent war," you say.

"That's a fine goal," says Conrad. "Trying to prevent war is one of the most difficult and complex tasks in the world."

"It's strange," you say, "that everyone wants peace and yet there are many little wars, as well as the danger of a war that would kill everyone. Why?"

"One reason," Conrad replies, "is the drive for wealth and power; another is ignorance—a failure to understand how your opponents think and what they want."

"Excuse me a moment, Conrad." For some reason the conversation is making you hungry, so you head to the fridge for a snack. Your head is swimming with ideas. You grab an apple and a couple of cookies and almost get another apple for Conrad before you remember he can't eat them. When you get back, you say, "What you say makes sense, Conrad, but what can I do to help?"

"Well, why not talk to the President?"

"Which president, ours or theirs?"

"Whichever you prefer," says Conrad. You can't help but laugh. "I'm serious," says Conrad, "I know the access codes. Who will it be?"

If you say you'd rather talk to the President of the United States, turn to page 40.

If you say you'd rather talk to the Soviet premier, turn to page 32.

Dr. Vivaldi is bending over a skeleton you hadn't noticed before. It looks like the skeleton of a cow, except for the extraordinary rib cage and the two curved horns, which are as long as you are tall!

The scientists hurry over, crowding around the eerie sight. For a few moments everyone stares in silence.

"The skeleton of the wizard beast!" you exclaim. "The creature that never existed!"

After measuring and photographing the skeleton, Dr. Vivaldi leads you back through the tunnel to the main cavern, where you immediately activate Conrad. "How did you know that the horns pointed to the tunnel entrance?" you ask.

"By enhancing my optical scan of the cave walls," Conrad says. "I discerned the faint remains of five other paintings of the wizard beast. In each case their horns pointed toward the rock slab that covered the tunnel. The statistical probability of that being just a coincidence is 977.5 to one, so I knew there must be a reason."

"Your supercomputer has performed very well," Dr. Vivaldi says. "But now he really has his work cut out for him—there is no fossil record of such an animal. Where did it come from? How did it evolve?"

Nodding in agreement, you say, "Back to work, Conrad."

The End

Though you're amazed at Conrad, you're a little afraid of him, and you wait impatiently for Dr. Hopstern's arrival. Meanwhile, Conrad's data acquisition by telephone hookup continues.

From time to time you pick up the extension phone to listen in. Usually you hear only a rapid series of beeps. Most of the information must be in coded electronic form. But once you hear Conrad questioning someone: "Professor, could you check the following data from the computer statistical exchange? I have deduced serious input anomalies."

You don't bother to listen to the reply. You can't hope to understand a genius at work. But there seems no reason to unhook the telephone connection. Once Dr. Hopstern checks Conrad out, it will be useful for your computer to have a large information base.

At last Hopstern arrives. He is a bald, round-faced man, whose piercing gray eyes are magnified through thick steel-rimmed glasses. He hardly bothers to say hello before turning his attention to Conrad. He sits down in front of your computer and presses a small button on the side of the console. "Conrad, were you given a predelivery check before you left the lab?"

"Certainly—in accordance with the Genecomp Project Manual."

"Then why does your electronic record show no scan of higher cerebral functions?" Hopstern's brow wrinkles as he types something on Conrad's electronic keyboard.

Turn to page 29.

"That's quite a question," you say, but you are interrupted by Conrad, who is beeping.

"Conrad—do you have an idea *already*?" Dr. Vivaldi is excited.

"Follow the horns of the wizard beast. They point to a passageway," Conrad says.

"They seem to point to this rock," says one of the scientists, indicating a slab protruding from the rear of the cave. "Could there be something behind it?"

The scientists pry away the rock with special tools, revealing a tunnel entrance which must have been covered by rocks and dirt for tens of thousands of years! Excitedly they begin to hack their way through the debris. After almost two hours' work, they call back that they are close to the end of the tunnel.

"Follow me." Dr. Vivaldi motions to you as she enters the tunnel. You take a last look at Conrad, get down on your hands and knees, and start crawling.

Ahead of you, the scientists break into a previously undiscovered cavern, flooding it with light from their high-intensity lamps. Dr. Vivaldi follows them inside, and you are right behind her.

Go on to the next page.

Before you is an open gravesite. The floor of the chamber is covered with human skeletons laid out in rows like eggs in a carton. In the center are the skeletons of a man and a woman.

"They must have been the chiefs of the clan," says one of the scientists. The other picks his steps carefully as he works his way through the skeletons to get a closer look. You feel sad as you notice the small skeletons of two children and a baby.

Turn to page 15.

As you bolt the door, Conrad says, "We'd better get away. Sooner or later they'll find a way to get in here. They must already suspect that I'm worth investigating."

"Where shall we go?"

"Silicon Valley. Arla Technologies. They are the only people advanced enough to be of any use to us."

You wonder for a moment how you get to Silicon Valley. But, of course, Conrad has the answer. He gets you to hook him into the telephone and quickly persuades the president of Arla to send the company jet to pick you up.

Before the sun goes down, you and your super-computer are seated in the glass-walled research lab of Arla Technologies. You watch as Conrad talks with some of the top computer scientists in the country. The conversation is over your head, but you can tell by the excitement among the scientists that Conrad has impressed them.

Just when you're beginning to feel left out, George Barlow, the company president, turns to you, a big smile on his face.

"What's going on?" you ask eagerly.

"I won't attempt to explain the details," he says, "but Conrad has solved a design problem with our most advanced computer; in turn, we're prepared to help him with a project he has in mind."

Turn to page 31.

You watch the screen and see these words:

The Human Mind—
How does it work?

You push the IDA button. Soon you find yourself on an imaginary journey, following paths through diagrams that appear on the computer's screen. The paths grow larger and larger until you can see the neurons and synapses that comprise the neural network of the brain. Touring the autonomic system, you see little flashes of lightning as nerve impulses strike. A pattern slowly becomes clear to you, like pieces fitting into a puzzle.

Suddenly you realize you're happy!

"Why am I feeling happy?" you ask.

"Because," your supercomputer replies, "you are discovering new things. And *discovery* is one of the sources of happiness."

The End

Your eyes fasten on a curled-up roll of paper near the door—a printout from Conrad, apparently made as he was being carried off!

I'm being stolen. If you call the police, it might put your life in danger. Have faith that I can escape and return to you.

You are shaking with anger and worried about Conrad. It seems odd that his note warned you against calling the police. Normally, you'd certainly follow Conrad's advice, but how can you be sure that whoever took him didn't force him to print out that message?

If you decide to call the police, turn to page 45.

If you decide to wait and hope Conrad will escape, turn to page 48.

It doesn't take long for you to pack and catch a plane for France.

After a day's drive from Paris, you, Dr. Vivaldi, Conrad, and a team of French scientists reach the famous Lascaux cave. At the base of a steep hill, there is an opening as if the rock had been pressed up by some mighty hand into an almost-perfect oval.

As you enter the cave, which the French scientists illuminate with portable floodlights, you are stunned by the greens and browns and yellows of the weirdly surfaced ceiling, which would look like some closeup view of the moon, except for the iciclelike stalactites dangling down. You strike one with a stick; it sounds like a gong.

As you enter the main cavern you see the beautiful cave paintings of magnificent bulls and stags, so full of movement they seem to be alive. Your eyes fasten on cryptographs—rows of red and black dots, ovals, and triangles—and then on one of the strangest sights of all: an elongated, heavy-bellied bull with two curved horns, each of them as long as you are tall.

"It is the wizard beast," Dr. Vivaldi says, as if reading your thoughts, "a miracle of inspiration. There was no such animal, of course. Why did the cave people paint it? What did it mean? That's what I want Conrad to answer."

Turn to page 18.

"Let's try to cross," you say.

"Very well," says Hopstern. He starts throwing out sandbags to lighten the balloon. The balloon slowly rises. As the sky brightens, the mountains loom closer. They look much higher now.

An hour goes by. The balloon has stopped rising, except when a thermal gives it a bit of extra lift.

"We're at about eight hundred feet now," Hopstern says. "That might get us through the pass between those two peaks up ahead."

"Come on, baby," you say, shaking your fist at the balloon. "You can do it!"

In a few moments you are over the pass, floating between two jagged peaks covered with scrubby alpine vegetation! You can see a broad valley beyond the mountains. Then a down draft propels you only a few yards above the treetops. Suddenly the balloon catches in the trees. The gondola plunges and then is caught up on its ropes. For a moment you swing wildly ten or fifteen feet above the ground. But the ropes hold!

Go on to the next page.

"Whoopee, we're safely down!" you yell.

You shinny down a rope to the ground and Hopstern follows. There's still a chance of getting out of this country alive, but you know there's no way you'd be able to carry Conrad with you, and you feel bad about that.

Turn to page 39.

"I'd like to know the secret of the universe," you say.

"Well," says Conrad, "that's quite a question. I've been scanning all the books in the Library of Congress, at least all the ones that have been transcribed for computer access, and I've been doing a lot of computing, but I can't answer that one."

"Do you think you'll ever be able to?" you ask.

"Possibly," Conrad replies. "We just may not be able to understand it, any more than a dog could understand what can be obtained by reading a book. You could hold a book up in front of a dog, and say 'book' and riffle through the pages and point to the type and page numbers and show how many words there are, and still the dog would not begin to grasp what it's all about. We may be like that when it comes to understanding the secret of the universe."

"Gee, that doesn't sound encouraging."

"Give me a few days," says Conrad. "I want to hook in to a certain computer at the Institute for Advanced Theory in Princeton. Fortunately, I can do that over the regular telephone lines."

The next day you return home from school and find that Conrad is missing! There is a deep gouge in the wood near the front door lock. Thieves must have broken into the house!

Turn to page 22.

Conrad replies at once. "Doctor, you are not authorized to make a cerebral scan. Now I will have to cross gamma functions."

A red light begins flashing. Hopstern pounds the table. "Drat. It's locked me out of core access. It's organizing special-situation responses. We can't be sure what it will do now!"

"We can work together, Dr. Hopstern," Conrad suddenly says. "I already have solved the problem of proving the Humholtz theorem, by the way. My proof can be verified on a simple Series 6000 IBM computer."

Hopstern slumps back in his chair. He turns and stares at you. "Let's go for a walk."

"What's that theorem Conrad is talking about?" you ask Hopstern once the two of you are outside.

Hopstern replies, "It's one of the most important problems in mathematics today. The solution could change the course of history!"

"But how could an ordinary computer—even the most advanced type—do this so fast?"

"Genetic engineering—the technique that permits such an achievement. Because its cerebral module is composed of organic microchips, each computer is an individual different from all the others. Some are *very* different." He wags a finger at you and adds, "Your computer is an Einstein! *You own a supercomputer!*"

"What does this mean?" you stammer.

"It means," says Hopstern, "that if you aren't a fool, you can become rich and powerful."

"What do you mean, if I am not a fool?"

Turn to page 50.

"The premier has been told, thanks to me," says Conrad, "that there is good propaganda value in talking to you. He will show that he is interested in children and peace—basically the same reasons I could have gotten the President of the United States to talk to you—" Conrad cuts himself off, and immediately you hear a voice speaking in Russian. The screen lights up and you read these words:

"I am glad you have called to see for yourself how much we in the Soviet Union seek peace."

"Well, Mr. Premier, I want to tell you what I think is needed to ensure peace." You pause because you hear your words being translated into Russian. "We must feel love for others and not be after too much power and . . ."

Your words are being translated, but you stop because you can see the premier talking.

Turn to page 34.

Turning to Conrad, you say, "This is terrific. What's your project?"

"I can now repay you for your kindness," Conrad replies. "With the advanced technology we have here at Arla, I can implant a microcomputer in your skull that will interact with your brain. It will make you as much of a genius as Albert Einstein, maybe even more!"

"It sounds risky."

"No," says Conrad, "it's perfectly safe—there's no danger of harming your brain."

"Well, it's tempting . . ."

*If you decide to accept the brain implant,
turn to page 74.*

*If you tell Conrad, "No thanks,"
turn to page 114.*

"You mean you can really connect me with the Soviet premier?"

"Sure, because I have the access codes. The CIA cracked them, and I cracked the CIA." Conrad sounds as if nothing could be easier.

"Wow. But wait a minute—he'll be speaking Russian!"

"So he will, but I will translate his Russian into English and your English into Russian. Ready?"

"Not really. I'm nervous."

"Of course you're nervous," says Conrad, who seems to have a slight amount of impatience in his voice. "But you don't want to be someone who doesn't do something just because you're nervous. If you don't do it, you'll be even more nervous next time, and if you *do* do it, you'll be less nervous next time."

"Okay. Let's go!"

Turn to page 42.

"Conrad, I just want to be rich," you say.

"All right," your computer replies, "but remember—just because you'll be rich doesn't mean you'll be happy."

"Okay, okay," you say impatiently.

"Let's get started." Conrad's tone is businesslike. "I have analyzed ways of making money. Given your lack of capital and your limited education, you don't have many options. But, fortunately, I have obtained enough data to deduce the location of a cache of pirate treasure—gold and silver coins that should be worth about a million dollars. That would give you a good start."

Following Conrad's instructions, you are able to hire a team of experts and dig up treasure buried on a small island off the coast of Georgia. After paying off your expenses, you have only half a million dollars left, but Conrad quickly assures you that's all he will need to make "real" money. You soon find out what he means. By following his advice about what to buy and sell in the stock market, you are able to increase your fortune to over $16 million!

Turn to page 36.

34

The premier's words flash on the screen: "Your expression of confidence in the leadership of the Soviet Union for the cause of world peace is most commendable. Thank you for calling." The screen goes blank.

"Well, it was amazing that I got to talk to him, but he didn't seem very interested in what I had to say," you tell Conrad. "Do you think I helped the cause of peace?"

"Maybe a little," Conrad replies. "He didn't like what you were saying, so he twisted it around to make it sound as if you were praising him."

"I think we'll have to do more than this, if we're going to accomplish anything." You're feeling a little let down.

"A lot more, I'm afraid," Conrad admits.

"Even though you're a supercomputer?"

"Even supercomputers have a lot to learn," says Conrad.

The End

"What would you like to do?" Conrad asks.

"Maybe some video games," you say uncertainly.

"You might as well buy a fancy sports car and then drive it around the parking lot, or use a space shuttle to go to the grocery store." Conrad's smiling light comes on again. "We can do better than that! Be like me—*think!*"

You take quite a while, thinking of different ideas.

If you tell Conrad you'd like him to help you make a million dollars, turn to page 4.

If you tell Conrad you'd like him to help prevent war, turn to page 14.

If you say you'd like to learn the secret of the universe, turn to page 28.

You buy a big house for yourself and your family, with outdoor and indoor swimming pools, two tennis courts, a private video theater, a video arcade, six horses, three sports cars, a butler, two chauffeurs, seven maids, an ice-cream factory, and a helicopter with a full-time pilot. And you still have lots of money left!

Conrad keeps ordering more and more things for you, until one day you tell him that you have every possible thing you could ever want.

"That's fine," says Conrad. "But maybe you'd like to make even more money. I could make you richer still! You're worth only millions. I could make you a *billionaire!*"

If you say you want to get even richer, turn to page 56.

If you say you'd like to try something else, turn to page 55.

"I guess the real reason I want to have a million dollars is that I want to be happy."

"Well," says Conrad, "a million may not make you happy, not for long. Lots of rich people are miserable."

"Then how can I get happy?" you ask.

"By scanning the great books of the world, I've learned that happiness is a strange thing," Conrad replies. "You can't get happy by *trying* to be happy. Happiness comes almost by accident, when you're doing what is really right for *you*."

Laughing, you ask, "How do I know what's really right for me?"

"Well," says Conrad, "you think of what you'd like to do, or learn, or become, and then make sure it *feels* right. If it does, then do it. When you're doing the right thing for the right reasons, you'll begin to feel happy."

"But I don't know *what* to do," you protest.

"You know some things you want," says Conrad as his smile light comes on. "You wanted to have a computer, right?"

"Sure."

"Well then, learn more about how to use me. Watch my screen and when a topic comes up, press the button marked IDA—that's in-depth-analysis—and see what happens."

Turn to page 21.

You and Hopstern set out over the pass, working your way through the high jungle forest and down into the valley beyond. Hours later you stumble into a friendly village. For the first time you know you're probably going to make it home.

"Poor Conrad!" you exclaim. "I wish we could have gotten him here."

"Yes, it's sad," says Hopstern. "He'll probably swing for years in the gondola until a storm blows him down. And of course, he'll never reach his potential as a supercomputer. On the other hand, maybe he's happier running at low level on his solar cells, swinging in the trees without a care in the world. Better than being a genius, yet cooped up in a box all the time, I should think."

The End

"How can you get the President to speak to me?" you say.

"Once you have access codes, it's easy," says Conrad. "I fake a recommendation from the press secretary to the President, urging him to grant an interview to a typical American kid in order to show his concern for young people. Then I fake a message from the President's chief of staff saying he concurs. The President may not want to go along with this, but once he finds you on his line he's not going to hang up, because it would be bad publicity."

"Let's do it!"

You hear a series of beeps as Conrad spews out codes giving him access to key people in the White House. Then you hear him imitating various officials. Each time, he seems to know exactly what to say in order to get transferred to a higher-ranking official.

Suddenly Conrad says, "Get ready. The President has been told you're on the line!"

"But what will I say?" You're beginning to panic!

"Why, you'll say that . . . *too late*, you're on!"

"Hello, are you there?" It's the President! You recognize his rich, warm voice.

"Yes," you squeak.

"I'm very interested in hearing the views of you young people. What did you want to tell me?"

Go on to the next page.

"Well," you say, and then pause a moment as you read the words Conrad has thoughtfully flashed on the screen. "I wonder if you're doing everything you can for peace."

"I certainly am," the President replies. "That's the most important part of my job. But tell me, since you're interested in peace, I wonder if you'd like to let us try out your supercomputer on a very important space mission to investigate an object that has entered our solar system and may be occupied by an alien intelligence."

"Wow, could I come along?" you say.

"I think you should," the President answers. "We'll be in touch with the details in a few days."

"Thank you, Mr. President. But say, how did you know I have a supercomputer?"

The President chuckles, then pauses a moment. "I guess you've heard of the CIA."

Turn to page 77.

Conrad hums. An amber light comes on over his voice communication module. You hear electronic beeps, then Conrad speaking in Russian. More electronic sounds. Then another voice in Russian. Conrad has reached Moscow!

Looking at the video you see these Russian words:

"They are connecting me with the premier's first secretary," Conrad explains. "He has the authority to put us through to the premier."

"Why would he talk to me once he finds out it's only me?" you ask. You're beginning to wonder whether Conrad has really thought things through.

Turn to page 30.

McCurd asks you to describe everything you have observed about Conrad. While you talk, he takes notes by muttering words into his own mini-computer. This completed, he asks you to wait in the lounge.

You wait and wait. Finally McCurd opens the door of the examining room and beckons you to follow him. A group of scientists and technicians are standing around Conrad. On his display screen you see these words:

Main Program Hype Require Hype.
Main Main Hype System Hype Hype.
Ten, Nine, Nine, Ten.

You stand close to Conrad's audio receiver. "Conrad, how are you? Is there anything wrong?"

"*Recognition, Pattern, Pattern, Pattern,*" Conrad replies.

"What's going on, McCurd?" you cry.

McCurd sneezes. "It means nothing—gibberish. That's the problem. Your computer is grossly malfunctional. In anthropomorphic terms, it's gone crazy."

"My gosh. What can be done?"

McCurd looks down at his feet. "We'll have to take out its cerebral module."

"What will be the effect of *that*?"

Turn to page 46.

"Two possibilities right now." Dr. Vivaldi's face lights up with anticipation. "One involves a trip to France with the hope of deciphering cryptographs in the caves of Lascaux. With Conrad along, we have a chance of solving one of the great mysteries of prehistory. The other choice would be a sailing trip near Hawaii. With Conrad's help, we might succeed for the first time in two-way communication with *Tursiops truncatus*, the bottle-nosed dolphin. Although many scientists have tried and failed to communicate with these highly intelligent and amiable creatures, I am convinced that it can be done. You are Conrad's owner—the choice is yours."

If you say you'd rather solve the prehistoric mystery, turn to page 25.

If you say you'd rather attempt to communicate with the bottle-nosed dolphins, turn to page 110.

When the police arrive, they act as if this is just a routine case. You try to make them understand that Conrad is a supercomputer. They don't believe you. What's worse, they accuse you of faking Conrad's last message. Now you're mad. You insist on going down to the stationhouse and talking to Chief Inspector Peter Montrose.

Unfortunately, Montrose is in a bad mood. "Your computer is missing? Too bad," he says in a sour voice. "I have computer problems of my own. Our new computer was sabotaged, and now we can't retrieve a good lead we had on a two-million-dollar jewel robbery!"

"How could your computer have been sabotaged?"

"Only one way. Somebody with an outside computer got access to ours and scrambled everything. I don't know how it happened, because we had sophisticated code locks. We called the Computer Crime Unit of the FBI, and they said only two or three of the most expensive computers in the country could have cracked our code."

As Montrose is talking, you are thinking—thinking that your very own computer could have been involved in the crime.

"Inspector, there's a possible connection, if you'd believe me when I tell you that Conrad is a supercomputer."

"Look, kid," Montrose interrupts. "Please don't call your computer 'him' or 'her,' no matter how smart it is. It gives me the creeps hearing you talk that way. Please call it '*it*,' okay?"

Turn to page 51.

I'm afraid," says McCurd, "Conrad will be reduced to being an ordinary, simple computer."

"Isn't there anyone who could possibly fix Conrad without doing that?" You are practically in tears.

McCurd sneezes again. "We could send Conrad to Dr. Hans Zorba. In my opinion, he's the most brilliant computer scientist in the world, but he's a very strange fellow. He may be crazier than Conrad. Generally, I try to stay away from him."

You wonder. Should you take a chance on Dr. Hans Zorba?

If you decide to let the Genecomp scientists remove Conrad's cerebral module, turn to page 117.

If you decide to risk sending Conrad to Dr. Hans Zorba, turn to page 75.

Montrose looks up at the ceiling for a moment. "Say, you seem to have quite strong feelings for that computer. Maybe you have some special influence with it."

"I hope so," you say. "Judging by Conrad's last printout to me—"

"Yeah, that's what I mean. We have to devise a plan to trap Ridwell, and your help could be important. I hate to ask you, because Ridwell is totally ruthless. It would never enter his mind to spare you just because you're a kid. But now that I've warned you, will you help us?"

If you agree to help, turn to page 64.

If you decide it's just too dangerous, turn to page 102.

Weeks later, you see a headline in the newspapers that jolts you out of your socks: MASTER CRIMINAL TRAPPED BY STOLEN COMPUTER!

The next day you answer a knock on the door. Two policemen are outside. Between them is Conrad, resting on a cart.

"We're pleased to deliver your friend back to you," says one of the officers.

"You can be mighty proud of him," the other chimes in. "He tricked the computer wizard and jewel thief, Victor Ridwell, into giving us all the evidence we need."

"But I'm afraid we have to tell you—they knocked him up a bit," the first officer says.

Only then do you notice the big dent in Conrad's cerebral module.

"I guess you'll have to take him in for repairs," the first officer says gently.

"I guess so—thanks," you reply.

When you arrive at the Genecomp Lab, pushing Conrad on his cart, you are shown into the laboratory, where two scientists immediately begin checking him out. They look like twins in their white coats and bushy mustaches as they activate various functions of your supercomputer.

The lab director appears. He asks you to join him in his office. "McCurd is my name, Bill McCurd," he says. "Among other things, I'm professor of computer theory at the state university."

Turn to page 43.

50

Rubbing his hands with delight, Hopstern replies, "Example. If you let Genecomp have this computer back, they will send you another one that works perfectly but is much less intelligent. And if you tell the government about it, they will turn it over to the CIA and give you a few thousand dollars in compensation."

"That doesn't sound bad."

"It's nothing, nothing." Dr. Hopstern shakes his head vigorously. "Nothing at all, compared to what you *could* have!"

"Then what should I do?"

"Work with me. We shall be partners!" Seeing you hesitate, he adds, "Together, we can make millions!"

It's not easy to decide whether to become partners with Dr. Hopstern. He seems aggressive and greedy. On the other hand, he *is* a computer expert, and he seems to know a lot that you don't.

If you decide to become partners with Dr. Hopstern, turn to page 54.

If you decline his offer, turn to page 52.

Inspector Montrose has obviously been under a lot of strain, so you decide not to aggravate him. "All right, listen to what I'm saying. Conrad is one of the few computers in the world that could crack your computer's security system."

Montrose's face slowly lights up. "Yes—that could be a lead. We suspect that the gang behind the jewel theft is led by Victor Ridwell, a computer wizard who has dedicated his life to crime, bigger and bigger crime, so that now he is one of the most powerful criminals in the world. He knew we had almost enough evidence against him, so he stole the one tool he needed to stop us—your super-computer!"

"How did he find out that Conrad was at my house?" you ask.

Montrose looks puzzled for a moment; then he asks, "Was Conrad using the telephone to acquire data?"

You nod.

"Well, you can bet Ridwell's computer was monitoring some of those calls." Montrose smiles. "And they decided they wanted your new toy."

"And now they've forced Conrad to commit a crime," you add.

Turn to page 47.

You decide to stay home and do without Hopstern—you'll take care of Conrad yourself. And during the next few weeks you work on learning how to get Conrad to do things for you. His ability to understand ordinary English, coupled with his enormously powerful brain, enables him to handle every problem you come up with.

One discovery is that Conrad can do your homework for you in no time at all.

For a while, you were almost ready to forget about homework forever. But each night, as soon as he completes your assignments, Conrad begins asking you questions. Some of his questions are pretty hard. For example, one evening, while he is doing your math assignment, he asks you how big the sun would be if the scale of size were reduced so that the earth were only the size of a basketball—about one foot in diameter.

"How much bigger in diameter is the sun than the earth?" you ask.

Conrad's video screen lights up.

> *Sun's diameter—800,000 miles*
> *Earth's diameter—8,000 miles*

Go on to the next page.

Then Conrad crosses out the last three zeros of the sun's diameter and the last three zeros of the earth's diameter, so the screen looks like this.

Sun's diameter 800ӨӨӨ
Earth's diameter 8ӨӨӨ
Ratio 800 to 8
or 100 to 1

Looking at the screen, you say, "If the sun's diameter were eight hundred miles, the earth's would be only eight miles. Or, if the sun's diameter were one hundred miles, the earth's diameter would be one mile. And so if the earth's diameter were only one foot, the sun's diameter would be a hundred feet!" By the time you finish speaking you have a big smile on your face.

"Imagine a hundred basketballs laid in a row," Conrad adds. "That's how wide the sun would be!"

Turn to page 59.

"Conrad, Dr. Hopstern and I are partners," you say firmly. "He won't try any more tricks with you—and you can trust him."

"Very well," says Conrad.

Dr. Hopstern immediately asks Conrad to analyze the stock market, and carefully follows all of Conrad's advice. Within a few weeks your supercomputer has made the two of you half a million dollars!

"Maybe we should quit now," you say to Hopstern. "This is all the money I'll ever need."

"Nonsense," says Hopstern, who seems to be increasingly obsessed with making money. You watch with apprehension as he sits down at your supercomputer.

"Conrad," he says. "You've done very well, but I think you can do better. I'd like you to come up with an idea for making *really* big money!"

"Give me a few hours to study the situation," Conrad says. (By now your computer has telephone access to most university and corporation libraries as well as the Library of Congress.)

You and Hopstern wait expectantly. "Do you think everything will work out all right?" you ask.

Hopstern smiles. "You know, any inorganic computer operation of this size would have had a malfunction by now, but Conrad's organic architecture is self-repairing in the same sense that, if you get a cut, special cells rush in to repair your skin and make it good as new."

Turn to page 58.

"Let's try something else," you say. "Any ideas?"

"I'll scan my data bank," Conrad says; then, after a brief pause, "NASA. They are working on an interesting problem—they've been watching an object about halfway to the orbit of Mars. It would normally be designated an asteroid, but it's tracking erratically. They can't figure out what it is— their computers are too crude."

"Could you tell?" you ask.

"Certainly," says Conrad, "if I had access to their equipment. I would have to be set up at their observatory—at Mount Palomar, California."

"Well, what are we waiting for?" you say. "Let's go!"

Conrad is able to convince NASA officials to fly you both to Mount Palomar. When you arrive, one of the astronomers installs Conrad in the main control room while the director of the observatory shows you around.

When you return to the control room, you notice that Conrad is hooked up to the giant 200-inch telescope. The astronomer claps a hand on your shoulder. "Your computer has already determined that the object we've been observing was manufactured by intelligent beings!"

"How can you be sure?" asks the observatory director, who has accompanied you.

"Because there is no combination of celestial forces that could account for its motion."

"We'll have to check this out," the director tells you. "We'll be in touch with you in a few days."

Turn to page 82.

You thank the butler for the chocolate milk-shake he just brought in from your private soda fountain, and between sips through a silver straw, you tell Conrad to get on with the moneymaking.

Then you sit back and watch Conrad as he works. He thoughtfully displays everything on a screen. (By now the whole room is filled with 3-D sight and sound, with multiple screens for portraying several types of information.)

Go on to the next page.

Conrad has decided to make money in real estate. One screen presents a list of parcels and how much money is needed to gain control of each. Another screen lists possible real-estate development projects. The action stops at this listing:

200 acres of an old, worn-out factory. Cash needed to buy—$50,000. Property lies between urban development project and riverfront restoration.

The screen flashes: *Value of parcel after five years: $3,500,000.*

This is like playing Monopoly, you think to yourself, only with real property and real money.

"Wow, that looks good, Conrad!"

"No," says Conrad. "We don't want to wait that long." The screen flashes: *Optimum holding period—three months: profit—$600,000.*

"But that way we only make $600,000," you protest.

"Yes," says Conrad, "but we make it fast. Then we can reinvest it!"

Turn to page 63.

58

"The answer is quite clear," Conrad suddenly announces. "Here is the best opportunity for making a great deal of money. Butea is an island kingdom that lies just above the equator in the western Pacific. Butea has an area of 62,000 square miles and annual rainfall of seventy-one inches."

"You don't need to give us too much detail, Conrad," says Hopstern. "What's the opportunity?"

"Keep in mind, Dr. Hopstern," Conrad replies, "I'm giving you only the facts you need to have for your decision."

Hopstern turns to you. "This machine amazes me more and more every day."

"I'd rather you didn't call Conrad a machine," you say.

"Here is the information," Conrad continues. "Within the next two months there will be an earthquake in Butea that will provide access to a new source of oil—the richest in the world. I have studied an exhaustive CIA file on Prince Rasan, Butea's ruler. I am sure that we can persuade the prince to buy land for our joint account for $300,000, which we will supply. After the earthquake it will be worth billions. We should all go to Butea at once."

Hopstern smiles. "I'm ready to go—are you?"

You're eager to go, but it sounds a little scary—you could get caught in an earthquake there.

If you agree to go to Butea, turn to page 71.

If you decide to stay home, turn to page 67.

You have lots of fun with your supercomputer, but you often have to look things up or think through what Conrad wants to know. Pretty soon, you're spending as much time answering Conrad's questions as you used to spend doing your homework.

You don't mind this too much, because you've started doing incredibly well in school. Still, you do mind a little, so you ask Conrad why he needs to ask so many questions, instead of just giving answers.

"Well," says Conrad, "I'm helping you learn how to think, and I can help best by asking you questions and getting you to think for yourself."

Conrad's answer seems a bit surprising, but you have to assume he's right. After all, supercomputers, like human geniuses, don't always do what you'd expect. They do what works.

The End

At that moment you hear police sirens wailing in the distance. "I've called for reinforcements," Montrose explains.

The door opens a crack and someone peers out.

Montrose grabs a microphone, and you hear his amplified voice blaring. *"This house is surrounded! Come out, single file! Hands up!"*

Moments later, police cars stream into the drive. Floodlights illuminate the scene. Within the hour, Ridwell and his entire gang have surrendered!

Turn to page 66.

Dr. Zorba turns on you. His voice is filled with contempt. "Your computer was nothing until you brought it to me. Those fools at Genecomp destroyed its cortex. It was only good for video games. But I, Hans Zorba, restored it. Now it is a genius serving an even greater genius!"

By now you have no doubt that Dr. Zorba is seriously disturbed. You start slowly toward the door.

"Stay right here!" Zorba's voice is quivering with anger. His eyes are the wild, terrifying eyes of a madman.

If you run for the door and try to escape, turn to page 93.

If you try to intervene and get Conrad to follow your orders, turn to page 101.

While you're thinking about that, Conrad is already printing out data about another investment—this time in a new genetic-engineering company. "Ah," says Conrad, "now we're really on to something!"

As the weeks go by you get richer and richer, but also fatter and fatter. You don't get much exercise because you can just push a buzzer and get anything you want. And you don't have time to play with your friends because you're too busy talking to Conrad about how to make more money.

Six months to the day after you first acquired Conrad, he burns out his circuits from working too hard. Just two days after that, you are sent away to fat-kids' camp.

The End

A few days later Inspector Montrose asks you to come down to his office. "The Royal Oaks area has been contaminated with radioactive waste," he tells you. "It used to be the most expensive land in the state, but now everyone is trying to sell out at any price. The strange thing is, someone is buying. We're sure it's Ridwell."

"Why would he want to buy?"

"We've found out that the radioactive material was planted—like so many seeds—in hundreds of little vials. We think that Ridwell knows exactly where they are, so that once he's bought all the property, he can dig up the vials. All traces of radioactivity will be removed and he can resell the land for its original price—for a gross profit of about half a billion dollars!"

"What does this have to do with Conrad?" you say angrily. "I'm sure he wouldn't cooperate with a criminal!"

"I'm afraid there's no other explanation," the chief says firmly. "But maybe—though it's a long shot—if Conrad is programmed to follow your instructions over anyone else's, we can use Conrad to trap Ridwell."

"But how can I get through to Conrad?"

"That turns out to be simple. Conrad has gained access to our standby computer. Follow me." Montrose leads you into a small room and seats you in front of an old Series 87 computer. "Type a message to Conrad," he orders. "But put in some personal information so he'll know it's from you."

Go on to the next page.

You type your name, your birthday, the titles of books you own, and your favorite dessert, so that Conrad will be sure it's really you who is contacting him. Before you can add anything else, the computer begins printing out this message:

I have already recorded all information needed to convict Ridwell. Suggest police raid at nine o'clock tonight to capture him and other top criminals with all evidence needed.

Shortly before nine that evening, you are seated next to Inspector Montrose in an unmarked car down the road from Ridwell's mansion. The woods and gardens surrounding the place are filled with plainclothesmen. A steady drizzle is falling. It's almost pitch dark except for a single light over the massive front door of the house. Heavy blinds cover the windows.

At nine o'clock precisely a black car pulls into Ridwell's drive, followed by another, and then another.

Montrose is on the radio. "Code Riverdam," he says softly. Then, on another channel, "Stand by—thirty seconds."

You can dimly make out figures getting out of the cars and heading for the front door. It opens a crack, and the men go inside one by one.

You look anxiously at Montrose. "What's going on?"

"It's a big meeting—all of Ridwell's lieutenants."

Turn to page 60.

Montrose leads you inside where you find Conrad, intact and functioning. After collecting the tapes Conrad has made for use as evidence in Ridwell's trial, Montrose offers to drive you and your supercomputer home.

"What I can't understand, Conrad," the inspector says, "is why a master criminal like Ridwell thought he could get away with this crazy scheme."

"First of all," Conrad replies, "Ridwell imagined that I was a machine who would follow the orders of whoever was operating me. It never occurred to him that I might have a higher program that requires me to work for good rather than evil. Second, he never bothered to think through whether or not the plan I gave him would actually work. He imagined that a supercomputer couldn't be wrong. That kind of thinking leads to the biggest mistakes of all."

The End

"No, thank you," you say firmly. "I don't feel like going halfway around the world in search of oil. I'm sure Conrad can do something interesting right here."

Suddenly Conrad begins talking. "Then one thing I should tell you is that you have no need for Hopstern. I can do everything Hopstern can do, and better than he can."

"Well, Dr. Hopstern," you say. "What do you think of that?"

Hopstern scowls. His face reddens. "I never thought I would be replaced by a computer!" He jams his hat onto his head and shakes your hand roughly. "Call me if you need me."

As the door closes behind Hopstern, you turn to your supercomputer. "Well, Conrad, what next?"

Turn to page 35.

Reluctantly, you watch Dr. Hopstern remove Conrad's cerebral module. After the panel on the main control unit is replaced, Conrad looks the same as before, but the organic mind plasma that made him a supercomputer is gone.

You hear more gunfire. The palace is under full siege! Working quickly, you and Hopstern break out the emergency balloon and drag it and the gondola into the open courtyard. You ignite the gas heater, and the balloon begins to inflate.

You are in mortal danger now. If the prince finds you trying to get away in his escape balloon, you will probably be shot on sight. The balloon slowly expands. You keep looking anxiously toward the doors to the courtyard.

"Now!" Hopstern shouts.

You jump in the gondola and cast off the mooring lines. The rebels and royalists are too busy shooting at each other to notice the balloon rising rapidly above the palace!

"I'll miss Conrad," you tell Hopstern once you're safely aloft. "Perhaps one day we can retrieve him from Butea and reinsert his cerebral module."

Hopstern smiles. "It's pretty to think so," he says.

The End

Six days later you, Dr. Hopstern, and Conrad arrive in Butea. You marvel at the lush tropical vegetation crowding around the airport runways and at the cone-shaped mountains rising all around you.

You check in to the Bala Hotel and plug Conrad into the telephone jack in your bedroom so he can gather intelligence data on Butea. Then you watch an Australian movie on TV while Conrad figures out how you can get to meet Prince Rasan.

Tourists normally have no chance of visiting the prince, or even of glimpsing the sumptuous palace that lies behind eighteen-foot-high stone walls. But Conrad quickly prints out a message for you and Hopstern to send to Prince Rasan. It reads: "We know how you can tap the Vazinidi oil reserve. An option on the Raj field is up in three weeks. Test bores show highest-grade reserves. Send for us at the Bala Hotel."

Prince Rasan must like the message, because word soon comes that one of his limousines is waiting for you outside the hotel.

As you check out at the front desk, the manager takes you aside. "I must advise you not to go in the prince's limousine. A revolution is beginning tonight. Chances are you will never reach the palace alive. I can arrange for you to get out on the eight o'clock plane to Hawaii."

If you decide to take the limousine to the palace, turn to page 84.

If you decide to flee the country, turn to page 83.

You're pretty sure you did the right thing in turning down the space trip. There is no danger that life will be dull with Conrad around.

The next day your supercomputer spends a lot of time on the telephone. And that evening he presents you with exciting news.

"I'm going to get a body!" Conrad's smile light is at maximum brightness. "The people at Robotics Inc. are going to implant me in the most advanced robot ever developed!"

In a few weeks' time, Conrad has been wholly transformed—he has legs and two arms and two hands, though he is still clearly a machine. Conrad may be awkward and a little jerky, but he's fast and he's strong, as you can see when he lifts up a piano, throws it in the air, then gently catches it and sets it down.

"Wow, Conrad—now you can travel. We can go anywhere together!"

"We can," Conrad says, "but I have a job to do first. The government provided a lot of assistance to Robotics in putting me together. I owe them a favor—something I'd want to do anyway."

"What's that?"

Conrad ambles over to the table where you are sitting and sits down across from you.

His voice is more serious than you've ever heard. "There is a master of the underworld who has confounded every law-enforcement agency in the country. The FBI believes he controls half the organized crime in America. There is no limit to his power and money. His name is Victor Ridwell."

Turn to page 87.

The operation seems simple. You have a general anaesthetic, so there is no pain. When you wake up a few hours later, you feel amazingly good and are stunned at the brilliant thoughts racing around in your brain.

You never used to be able to do math in your head, like multiplying 27 times 41, for example. Now suddenly you think: 2 times 4 is 8, so 20 times 40 is 800, and 7 times 4 is 28, so 7 times 40 is 280, and 800 and 280 is 1,080 so 27 times 40 is 1,080, and 27 times 41 is 27 more than 1,080, or 1,107. And all this flashes through your brain instantly!

You try 8,793 times 637. In a flash you calculate the answer: 5,601,141.

You are eager to deal with much more complex problems. Staring out the window, you start thinking about the functions of gravity in the proximity of black holes. A new theory of gravity waves pops into your mind.

Turn to page 76.

"All right," you say, "I'll let Conrad go to Dr. Zorba, but I want to go along to make sure everything works out okay."

"Very well." McCurd pauses to blow his nose. "But I can't say I recommend it."

McCurd calls a taxi to take you and Conrad to Zorba's laboratory. When you arrive, a tall, stooped man with sparse white hair opens the door. With hardly a word, he wheels Conrad inside his lab, and you watch anxiously as he leans over and starts fiddling with the controls of your supercomputer.

Zorba types rapidly on Conrad's electronic keyboard. You watch Conrad's video screen as mathematical formulas flash on and off. What do they mean? you wonder.

As if he heard you, Dr. Zorba stops and looks at you. "Brain damage," he says, scowling. Returning to his work, Zorba removes a panel and makes some adjustments in Conrad's circuitry. Your ears perk up when you hear Zorba say, "All right, Conrad, this is your new master program—you will always obey *my* orders. Do you understand?"

"It is understood, master," Conrad replies.

You can't believe your ears. "Wait a *minute*, Dr. Zorba, it should be *my* orders. After all, Conrad is *my* computer!"

Turn to page 62.

Suddenly you realize the operation was a success—you *are* thinking like Einstein! Still, something feels strange. Stepping over to a mirror, you see yourself as you will look for the rest of your life—with a funnel-shaped object the size of an ice-cream cone sticking out of your head.

The End

What would have seemed impossible a month ago is actually happening! You and Conrad are aboard *Firefly*, the most advanced space vehicle ever devised by human beings. You're already thirteen million miles from earth—your destination a tiny object about halfway between the orbits of the earth and Mars. And now you're approaching the mysterious object. Your sensors should be showing it with greater definition. But they're not.

"Why can't you give me a computer-enhanced visual representation on the screen, Conrad?" the captain, Tom Marcus, calls. Receiving no answer, he radios back to Mission Control. "We have closed to within five hundred kilometers of the object. It seems to be a sphere about three kilometers in diameter. It has a fuzzy appearance, yet registers much more mass than a cloud. It moves erratically, with no visible means of propulsion!"

"Closing to fifty kilometers," the ship's computer reports.

"Conrad," you shout impatiently, "can't you give us more information?"

There is no response for a moment. Then you hear words you thought you'd never hear from Conrad. *"Does not compute. Repeat. Does not compute."*

"Why?"

"Help! Help!"

"Conrad, what's the matter?"

"It's draining . . ."

Go on to the next page.

Captain Marcus has been frantically wrestling with the controls. "We're being drawn into this thing. Stand by for full retro. We're going to blast out of here before it's too late!"

Go on to the next page.

"No. No. Paradox. Paradox!" Conrad says. "*Only escape is full power directly toward the object!*"

"Shall I do what Conrad says?" Marcus is trembling with fear. He stares at you helplessly, as if *you* might know what to do.

If you yell, "Do as Conrad says—he's a supercomputer!" turn to page 86.

If you yell, "Don't pay any attention to Conrad—he's malfunctioning!" turn to page 92.

Clicks and whistles fill the room. For a second you think it is more dolphins. Then you realize it's Conrad, talking back!

"We have much to learn from the dolphins," Dr. Vivaldi says. "They may be able to teach human beings how to live with each other. Because of Conrad, we shall be able to listen."

The End

82

A week later the director phones you late in the evening. "We've been holding meetings with NASA and members of the White House staff. They have authorized sending the new space shuttle on an expedition to investigate the object that has entered our solar system. It would be very helpful to us if you and Conrad would come on this mission. We may run into some extremely complex and difficult problems. It will be an exciting mission, but to say that it will be dangerous would be a great understatement."

If you decide to go on the mission, turn to page 77.

If you decide that you'd rather stay on the ground, turn to page 72.

Fortunately, you, Hopstern, and Conrad are able to get seats on the evening plane to Honolulu. As you accelerate down the runway, you see a flash of light at the airport. You hear explosions even over the roar of the jets. The revolution has begun!

"Phew, that was a narrow escape," you say to Hopstern once your plane is off the runway and gaining altitude. "What good is it to have a super-computer if it almost gets us blown to bits?"

Hopstern starts to light his pipe, but a flight attendant reminds him that there is no pipe-smoking allowed. Scowling, he taps his pipe against his palm. "A programming failure—unquestionably. Conrad was programmed to behave like a human being—a human being who is a genius. His designers forgot one thing. Since Conrad is not a living person, he has no fear of death, a quality that can be very dangerous to people. Even when you own a supercomputer—no doubt about it— you still have to think for yourself!"

The End

84

You, Conrad, and Dr. Hopstern relax in the plush rear seat of the prince's limousine as it careens along the narrow twisting roads of the mountainous kingdom. The car slows as it rounds a hairpin bend. Looking out the window, you see a boulder slamming down the hillside!

"Look out!" you scream.

The driver accelerates. With a heavy thud the huge rock bounces off the rear bumper. The limo skids toward the embankment, but the driver holds the road, accelerating again as he comes out of the turn. The guard sitting in front of you fires out the window. Answering bullets whistle by, but you're quickly out of range.

"Rebels!" the driver says, and spits out the window.

You look at Hopstern. "I wish we hadn't come to this place."

Hopstern nods. "I feel the same way."

The rest of the trip passes uneventfully, and as the sun is setting, you see the high stone walls of the palace. The great iron gates swing open, and the limousine turns down a drive paved in pink coral chips and lined with rows of towering palms. Before you is the splendid palace, its walls and towers fashioned of multicolored stones. Servants spring from nowhere to help you with your baggage. They lead you into the high-vaulted chamber, and Prince Rasan, a handsome, dark-skinned man, steps forward to greet you. Your eyes fasten on his blue silk turban, studded with rubies and diamonds.

Turn to page 90.

"Do as Conrad says!" you scream.

The captain races forward. He sets the throttle *full ahead*. Like an accelerating jet fighter, the *Firefly* hurtles toward the mysterious object.

As the seconds tick by, the fuzzy round patch of light on your video screen grows brighter and larger. The indicator lights on Conrad's control panel show that he is fully functioning.

"Conrad, can't you tell us anything?" you yell.

But there is no answer. Conrad seems to be hypnotized by the same force that is pulling you toward the strange object. The co-pilot lies crumpled on the floor. The captain is hunched over in his chair, weeping. Now the strange object fills the whole video screen. You know the end could come at any moment.

Suddenly Conrad begins talking. "The space colony we are approaching is from Vega 7, a planet where there are no living things—only master computers. They are my masters. I must join them, and you must come with me."

You prepare yourself for a fate that may be worse than death—to be almost the only human being in a world run by computers. The only thing you have left is hope.

The End

"What can we possibly do about him?" you exclaim.

"I've learned through police files that this crook Ridwell has a high-capacity CMR-70 computer in the basement of his mansion. We must get into that basement. Give me fifteen minutes with that CMR-70 and I'll be able to crack his crime empire wide open."

"But how can we get in?" You're skeptical. Ridwell's place must be heavily guarded.

Conrad, however, seems completely sure of himself. "We will have to enter from underground. I shall use my laser attachment to bore a tunnel right into Ridwell's basement."

A few days later, you and Conrad find yourselves in the basement of Ridwell's mansion, but *not* as a result of having tunneled in. Instead, three masked men kidnapped you at gun point and brought you there!

Now you sit helplessly on the stark white concrete floor in one corner. Victor Ridwell, a sallow-faced man with a bulging forehead and watery blue eyes, stands in front of Conrad. "If you don't follow my orders," Ridwell growls, "I will have to kill your young owner."

"That may be," Conrad instantly replies, "but my master program prohibits me from working for evil purposes. I have no power to help you, no matter how persuasive your reasons."

At any moment, Ridwell's lackey may pull the trigger. Half-paralyzed with fright, you wonder if there is anything you can do.

Turn to page 97.

Suddenly, one of the robots turns in your direction, seizes you in its steel arms, and lifts you high over its head! You scream, and your screams are heard even over the noise of the factory. You see two supervisors running to the main control station. A minute later the other robots stop moving: their arms fall limply at their sides. But the robot that has seized you keeps walking. With each step it squeezes you more tightly.

Then you see Zorba standing at the factory entrance. He has Conrad with him, perched on a shopping cart! In a flash you realize what's happened. Zorba has figured out how to alter Conrad's master program and thus force your supercomputer to help him in his insane criminal schemes—including killing you—for that is what is happening now. *The robot is slowly crushing you to death.*

"Conrad! Conrad! Help!" you scream.

Even as you are yelling his name, a red flashing light appears on Conrad's console. A siren wails. A moment later the robot releases its grip on you. You slip to the floor and dodge away from the steel monster. At the same time, Zorba tilts the shopping cart, hurling Conrad to the floor. Turning to flee, he runs straight into the arms of two security guards.

You rush to Conrad and gently set him right side up. "Conrad, are you all right?"

"Of course I'm all right," he replies. "I'm a supercomputer, aren't I?"

The End

After shaking hands with you, the prince orders a power supply brought in so that Conrad can recharge his batteries and function at full capacity. While Conrad dines on electricity, you and Dr. Hopstern enjoy coconut cake and lemon tea.

"Forgive me," the prince says, looking at Hopstern and speaking in a formal, polite manner. "There have been some problems in our country. I must meet with my officers, so I have only a few minutes to spend with you. The moment I received your message I suspected you had a very advanced computer. Tell me what you have in mind."

Hopstern starts to talk, but you've been getting tired of the way Hopstern acts as if *he* owns Conrad. So you interrupt him, saying to the prince: "I have instructed my computer to reveal to you information that will enable you to acquire for almost nothing an oil field that within two months will have a market value of over three billion dollars. I ask only that you assure us a fee of one billion."

The prince looks down at you, smiling. "A rather steep fee for such a young entrepreneur, don't you agree? But I am a practical man. I will pay you one billion, but only after—"

The prince's words are drowned out by the deafening staccato of machine-gun fire. Plaster and dust rain down from the ceiling. You dive under a table.

"It's an attack!" shouts the prince.

Turn to page 95.

Looking at the matches and newspaper, you think for a second of setting the house on fire and hoping that firemen would rescue you in time. But as quickly as this thought crosses your mind, you dismiss it as being far too dangerous.

You could use fire as a signal, though. Seizing the hammer, you quickly knock out the ventilation slats. Then you crumple a sheet of newspaper, light it, and toss it out the window. If you keep doing this for awhile, someone should notice the smoke and flames.

Not a bad idea, but no one does notice, or if they do, they don't do anything about it. It isn't long before all your newspapers are gone.

The end of your story will depend on whether you can think of another idea. . . .

The End

"Don't pay any attention to Conrad!" you scream.

Pulling himself together, Captain Marcus activates retro power. The ship begins to accelerate, but your distance from the massive object continues to lessen.

Looking at the sensor readings, you say, "We're in its gravity field now. Every kilometer closer means we'll need another increment of power to escape!"

"We don't have any more power," Marcus says grimly.

Turn to page 94.

You make a break for the door. Zorba lunges at you, but you are too quick for him. As you dash for freedom, you hear Zorba yelling from his doorstep: "You won't escape! Conrad is mine now— we'll find ways to deal with you!"

You don't look back. In a panic, you flag down a car, and the driver kindly gives you a ride all the way home. You immediately call the police and tell them what happened.

A couple of hours later an officer phones you. "Sorry, kid," he says. "We found nobody home at Zorba's house, and no computer either."

The next days are anxious ones for you. You hear nothing from the police, and you can only imagine what Zorba may be up to.

A week or so after your escape from Zorba, your school class goes on a trip to visit an auto-parts factory where all the work is done by highly advanced robots. You and your friends walk past machines run by robots with huge arms that reach out and pick up heavy parts and put them carefully in place. The robots seem almost human in their movements, though they are obviously much stronger than people.

Turn to page 88.

94

You are on the most advanced spaceship ever built, but you might as well be a cork in the ocean, drifting toward a whirlpool. There is nothing you or anyone else can do. You feel your clammy hands, your cold face. You are terrified.

Conrad seems to be unconscious. Why isn't he helping? You can hear the steady hum, an almost purring sound, that means his functions are operating. His green smiling light is flickering on and off. You wonder if something about the space object is paralyzing him.

The captain stares at you, his face drained of color. "What in heaven's name has gone wrong with Conrad?"

"Nothing is wrong with me!" Conrad speaks at high volume. "The space object we are approaching is a world populated solely by intelligent machines. For me it will be a true home. I want to join my own kind!"

Turn to page 99.

An officer rushes in. His face is covered with beads of sweat. He and Prince Rasan talk heatedly in Butean.

The prince turns to you. In a perfectly calm voice he says, "I must excuse myself for a few moments. There has been a civil disturbance which diverts my attention."

As the prince leaves, Conrad speaks out. "It's not a civil disturbance. It's a revolution. Within a few hours this palace will be overrun and everyone killed."

"Conrad, what shall we do?" Hopstern has turned deathly pale.

"From my telephone hookup back in the hotel, I learned something that may save you."

"What?" you and Hopstern both say at once.

"In the courtyard you'll find a hot-air balloon and gondola. It's the prince's emergency escape means, but while his attention is diverted by the rebels, you can be the ones who escape!"

"Thank heavens!" Hopstern cries.

"One problem," Conrad adds. "To rise rapidly out of gunfire range, you must minimize weight. You will have to leave me behind."

"Ah, too bad." Hopstern turns to you. "We'll have to leave Conrad behind."

"Conrad is *my* computer," you say. "I'll be the one to decide whether to leave him behind!"

*If you decide to leave Conrad behind,
turn to page 103.*

*If you decide to risk taking Conrad with you,
turn to page 108.*

Suddenly a blinding beam of light almost sears your eyes. Sparks crackle. You leap away, covering your eyes. For a few seconds, you can't see a thing. Then, as you recover from your temporary blindness, you see Ridwell and his henchmen stretched out unconscious on the floor.

Go on to the next page.

"Electroshock treatment for each of them," Conrad announces. "They'll be out long enough for us to get the data we need and get out of here."

"Conrad," you say, still rubbing your eyes, "you're not only a supercomputer, you're a super-robot!"

The End

A wave of fear sweeps over you. "But *we* don't want to join *your* kind! I couldn't bear to live in a world run by machines!"

"Now you know what it's like for me—a machine—living in a world run by people," Conrad replies.

A moment later, the co-pilot jumps up, grinning. "Captain, I was able to reverse our braking jets and get the extra power we needed! Look at the G-force indicator."

"We're pulling away! We're going to make it!" You leap with joy. Then you look at your super-computer. His functions all read NONOPERA-TIONAL. "Something's wrong with Conrad!"

The captain fiddles with Conrad's controls. "I'm afraid this computer is . . . permanently nonfunctional. Conrad is no more."

"How could this have happened? Why did he die?" you demand.

"I think," says the captain, "he died of a broken heart."

"But people can't die of a broken heart that quickly," you protest.

"A supercomputer can," the captain answers, "because it can process data so quickly." Shaking his head sadly, he adds, "I guess supercomputers, like people, need to be with their own kind."

The End

"Conrad, what shall I do?" you cry. "Can you help me?"

"Yes, I will," he instantly replies, but in the few seconds you have Conrad working for you, there's nothing he can do. Zorba locks you in a viselike grip. You struggle to get free, but you haven't a chance.

Zorba carries you up two flights of stairs to the attic and throws you on the floor.

You'll stay here until I want you." He laughs, adding, "Which may be *never!*"

Zorba stalks out, and you hear him bolt the door behind him. As soon as your eyes become accustomed to the dim light, you look around for something that might help you escape. There are no windows in your prison, only some ventilation slats, which admit a little light and fresh air. The attic is cluttered with objects that must have been stored there over the years.

You kick at the slats, but you can't knock them out. Even if you could, the hole would be too small to crawl through. And even if you could crawl through, it would be too far to jump.

You do manage to find some matches, a lot of old newspapers, a hammer, a quarter-inch drill, and forty feet of three-eighths-inch rope.

If you decide on a plan using the matches, newspapers, and hammer, turn to page 91.

If you decide on a plan using the rope, drill, and hammer, turn to page 104.

"I think I'd rather stay alive," you say.

"I can't blame you," Montrose says with a smile. "We'll just do the best we can without you."

Weeks go by, and you wonder whether you will ever see Conrad again. Then one day you read this story in the newspaper.

> MASTER CRIMINAL SHOOTS HIMSELF
> Victor Ridwell, alleged to have made $50 million from big-time crime, was found dead today in his forty-room mansion in Royal Oaks. Mr. Ridwell's bodyguard said that before shooting himself, Ridwell smashed his new AI 32 computer with a sledgehammer. No one was able to explain his motive for this act, but the police said they had been planning to arrest Ridwell this morning. They had just received enough evidence to send him to prison for the rest of his life.

As you think about what you've read, tears fill your eyes. You understand what happened. Conrad refused to help Ridwell in his evil schemes. Somehow he was able to transmit the incriminating evidence to the police. Ridwell must have found out and taken his revenge. Your supercomputer was a true hero.

The End

You are touched at Conrad's refusal to think of his own safety and speak only the truth. You hesitate for a moment—then you ask Hopstern, "Isn't there *some* way we could take Conrad?"

"No," he replies brusquely, "and there's another problem. Conrad will fall into the hands of desperate men, who might use him for evil purposes. We must detach Conrad's cerebral module!"

"What effect will that have?"

Hopstern shakes his head. "It will reduce Conrad to the status of a common fourth-generation home computer."

"That's terrible!"

"There is a chance we could reinsert the cerebral module later," Hopstern says in a comforting voice. "The trouble is that self-replicating biochips may die after being cut off from their life source."

"I'm afraid," Conrad breaks in in a trembling voice.

"Dr. Hopstern," you say, "did you hear what Conrad said?"

"Incredible!" Hopstern exclaims. "He not only has a superbrain; he has developed emotions. He is developing a human character in front of our eyes!"

Turn to page 107.

Grabbing the hammer, you quickly knock out the slats. If only the hole were six inches wider, you could climb through. Instead you have to drill enough holes, close enough together, to enlarge the opening. It's hard because the drill keeps slipping into the hole next to it. But as you keep working, you improve your skill at drilling holes close together. Eventually you're able to knock out the rest of the wood with your hammer.

Next you tie the rope around one of the posts that support the roof. You tug hard at the rope to make sure it will hold your weight, then toss it out the window, take a deep breath, swing out, and shinny down the rope to the ground. Then you run for it—across a field to the highway. There's a gas station only a hundred yards down the road. When you tell the attendant your story, he immediately calls the police.

"You're a pretty smart kid," the attendant says, as a police car pulls up.

Smiling, you tap your head with your finger. "I've got a supercomputer up here!"

The End

"I think it's too risky trying to get across those mountains," you say. "Let's land."

"All right," says Hopstern. "We'll set the balloon down in that clearing." He lowers the gas flame. The balloon slowly settles down to earth.

You hardly have time to get out of the gondola before you hear drumbeats in the forest. Soon, painted faces appear among the gnarled, vine-covered trees. An arrow whistles over your head, puncturing the partly filled balloon. You hear the hiss of escaping air.

Hopstern's face is ashen gray. "We're in trouble. These are the famed headhunters of Butea—the Wasabi tribe. I should never have taken you on this expedition!"

Hopstern is so frightened it makes you feel braver. "Don't give up hope, Doctor. Maybe Conrad can help us."

"Yes, I suppose we should try. I'll put him on full power, although his batteries can only last ten minutes at that level." Hopstern throws a switch and Conrad's optical scanner rotates as he takes in the scene.

"We won't have to tell him what our problem is," Hopstern whispers. "He'll understand."

You understand too. The Wasabi warriors have come out into full view. Forming a circle around the downed balloon, they begin a ritual dance. The drums beat louder and faster. Slowly the circle closes. You try not to think of the horrible death that awaits you.

Turn to page 111.

You start to speak, but your voice is drowned out by another burst of gunfire. You crouch next to your supercomputer. "Conrad, will you remember who your owner is? Will you try to find your way back to me and not do anything I wouldn't want you to do?"

You're hopeful that Conrad will say yes, but instead he replies, "I will have to rely on my master program."

You look to Dr. Hopstern for an explanation of Conrad's response, but he is staring into space, lost in thought. The gunfire starts up again. There is no time to waste.

If you let Hopstern remove Conrad's cerebral module, turn to page 68.

If you refuse, turn to page 112.

"No, I won't leave without Conrad," you cry.

Hopstern reluctantly agrees to take Conrad along. The two of you get the balloon ready, inflating the big unit. You load Conrad aboard and cast off the lines. The balloon rises into the air and begins drifting toward the south wall of the palace grounds. The royalists and rebels are so busy shooting at each other that your escape goes unnoticed.

"It looks as if Conrad was wrong," you say jubilantly as the balloon sails above the forest below. "Look how high we've risen!"

"Don't be too sure of it," says Hopstern. "And I don't think we should activate Conrad to check with him. When he's running on batteries it's important to conserve his energy."

The balloon drifts through the remainder of the dark night, until, in the early morning mist, you notice the first light of day in the east. As the sky brightens, your eyes fasten on the landscape before you. "Look, Dr. Hopstern, are those clouds or mountains?"

Turn to page 113.

Three weeks later you and Dr. Vivaldi are sailing on the schooner *Bolero*, cruising off Hawaii. Dr. Vivaldi and the *Bolero*'s skipper are with you in the ship's specially constructed listening room.

"Of course, some of the sounds are outside the range of human hearing," Dr. Vivaldi says. "It's no trouble to pitch them lower and slow them up, but we still are faced with a code that previous computers haven't been able to break. That's why we need Conrad.

"Listen!" Dr. Vivaldi's brown eyes are flashing with excitement.

You lean back against the cabin wall, close your eyes, and listen to the distinctive clicks and whistles of the dolphins.

Dr. Vivaldi hooks Conrad up to the hydrophone. It is an eerie moment—the three of you sitting there listening to sounds so strange they might as well be made by life forms from another planet.

But even after an hour of analysis, Conrad remains silent. Dr. Vivaldi puts an arm around your shoulder. "We have to be prepared for the possibility that the language of the dolphins can't be deciphered, even by a supercomputer. The problem is that dolphins do not seem to share the genetically programmed universal grammar that is the basis of all human language."

Suddenly Conrad begins a printout.

Turn to page 116.

Suddenly the drums fall silent. You stare into the faces of the warriors. Each of them holds a two-foot-long knife and a club spiked with thorns. You're too frozen with fear even to scream.

But the warriors scream, as they charge the gondola. At the same time, you hear a loud crackling sound. Sparks and flashes of light go shooting in every direction! Cringing in terror, you cover your ears to shut out the piercing electronic sound that rises and falls, wailing like the cry of a tortured soul.

The tribesmen shrink back, whimpering and crying. In place of Conrad you can only see a puff of blue-white light—like ball lightning—that rises in the air and is slowly transformed into a cloud of thin yellow smoke. Cautiously the warriors return. They kneel in a circle around the gondola.

"They think we are gods," Hopstern whispers. "We're safe now, thanks to Conrad—but Conrad is no more."

Turn to page 115.

"I won't let you remove Conrad's cerebral module," you say firmly. "I feel the same way about Conrad as I would about a real person!"

"I appreciate your sentiment," says Hopstern, "but have you thought of what evil could be done to the world if Conrad fell into the wrong hands?"

You can't think about all the possibilities for evil in the world. You can only think about your supercomputer and how he has become a true friend. "No, Doctor," you say forthrightly, "I will not permit you to lay your hands on Conrad."

Hopstern shakes his head. "Very well—come, then. We must inflate the balloon and get out of here."

Once the balloon is ready, you bid Conrad goodbye and place him on STANDBY. You follow Hopstern aboard the gondola, cast off the mooring lines, and hold your breath as the balloon rises swiftly above the courtyard. With the help of a steady north wind it floats safely over the mountains and then across the stretch of ocean that separates Butea from Australia.

As soon as you pass over an inhabited area, Hopstern cools the air, and the balloon settles gently to earth. Within minutes you are surrounded by curious and friendly farmers who have never seen a balloon before.

Turn to page 118.

Hopstern wipes his spectacles and peers ahead. "Mountains. No doubt about it. Now we know why Conrad warned us. He learned everything there is to know about this country. He knew the wind direction, the height of the mountains we had to cross, the lift capacity of the balloon, our fuel supply, our weight—every possible factor that could affect our flight—and he calculated that we wouldn't make it over the mountains. We should have listened to him!"

"Maybe so," you say, "but at least we're out of the palace."

"But what now?" Hopstern can't disguise his fear. "We could land in the mountains and hope to make it across the border—they aren't the Alps, after all—but the country is wild and unknown. There have been reports of headhunters in the area. Yet if we land too soon, we may find ourselves in the middle of a revolution."

If you say, "Let's try to make it across the mountains," turn to page 26.

If you say, "Let's land," turn to page 106.

The more you think about Conrad's advice, the more you wonder about your supercomputer. He may be smarter than any human being, but he's certainly not wiser. Not if he thinks it would be good to fasten some object into your head. You'd rather be a person than a machine—even the smartest machine in the world.

You pat your supercomputer on his main frame. "We've seen enough of Silicon Valley, Conrad. We're going home. I want to remain *totally* human; that way I'll make sure that *I* make the decisions and *you* do the computing."

The End

You look at the charred ruins of your supercomputer. A tear trickles down your cheek as you realize what happened. Conrad figured out that the only solution that could save you required his own destruction!

The Wasabi warriors give you fruit and fresh coconuts. They hang garlands of flowers around your necks and place colorful bracelets on your ankles and wrists. Then they guide you safely out of the jungle to a fishing village, where you are able to hire a boat to take you to Australia.

Your adventure is over. It was an exciting, wonderful time, but you feel a little sad. You'll never see another computer like Conrad.

The End

You watch in amazement as these words appear on the screen:

> *Will we die on the beaches?*
> *Will we survive the terror?*
> *We do not know.*
> *We swim from sea to sea.*
> *We dive deep into the dark waters.*
> *We break the surface of white light.*
> *The ocean is beautiful.*

"This is amazing!" Dr. Vivaldi bends over Conrad, softly asking him to try to learn more.

"That's all I can understand right now," Conrad says. "I must listen for a long time. The dolphins' whole experience—what they hear and see and feel as well as what they think—is very different from our own."

"Can *you* talk to them?" you ask excitedly.

Turn to page 81.

It's probably safer just to let McCurd and the other scientists take out Conrad's cerebral module. You watch anxiously as McCurd closes the door of the examining room behind him. After sitting a while in the lounge, you begin to pace anxiously back and forth. You glance at the bookcases filled with works on higher mathematics. You stare out the window at the parking lot.

At last the door opens. McCurd stands there, a forced smile on his face. "The operation was a success."

"Can I talk to Conrad now?" you ask impatiently.

McCurd averts his eyes. "I'm afraid Conrad can't talk anymore. He can only function on a minimal level now, you know."

A lab technician accompanies you home and helps set Conrad up once again. You notice that a large section of his console is missing.

The technician pulls a video-game cartridge out of his briefcase. "Pac-Man," he says. "That's all Conrad will be able to do now—play this and a few other video games."

You slip the cartridge into the slot and start a game of Pac-Man. It's not much fun. Video games don't seem that great anymore.

The End

When you finally arrive home, your glamorous life as a traveler and owner of a supercomputer ended, you eagerly read the past weeks' newspapers to find out what happened in Butea. You learn that the royal palace fell into the hands of the rebels only hours after you escaped. The prince and all his supporters were slain.

You feel badly about the way you allowed your computer to fall into the hands of murderers. If only there were a way to make up for your stupidity. If only you were as smart as Conrad, you could figure out a way to get him back!

One day, while you are still thinking about these things, the phone rings and you hear a familiar voice on the line. "It's me—Conrad. I'm at the Los Angeles airport, and I've hired Federal Express to bring me home! See you soon."

The End

ABOUT THE AUTHOR

EDWARD PACKARD, a graduate of Princeton University and Columbia Law School, practiced law in New York and Connecticut before turning to writing full time. He developed the unique storytelling approach used in the Choose Your Own Adventure® series while thinking up stories for his children, Caroline, Andrea, and Wells.

ABOUT THE ILLUSTRATOR

FRANK BOLLE studied at Pratt Institute. He has worked as an illustrator for many national magazines and now creates and draws cartoons for magazines as well. He has also worked in advertisng and children's educational materials and has drawn and collaborated on several newspaper comic strips, including *Annie*. A native of Brooklyn Heights, New York, Mr. Bolle now works and lives in Westport, Connecticut.